August "92"

Dear Christopher,

Cincinnati Zoo
with Uncle Tim, Aunt Elli,
Michael, and mom. You
had a wonderful time.

Love you,
mom & Dad
X X X O O O

Adapted and published in the United States in 1986
by Silver Burdett Company,
250 James Street, Morristown, New Jersey
in association with Belitha Press Ltd., London

**Library of Congress Cataloging-in-Publication Data**
Hoffman, Mary, 1945–
　　Animal hide and seek.

　　(Let's read together)
　　Summary: When a family goes to the zoo, only the children
seem to be able to see the animals, camouflaged by their
natural setting.
　　[1. Zoo animals–Fiction] I. Baxter, Leon, ill. II. Title.
III. Series: Hoffman, Mary, 1945-　　. Let's read together.
PZ7.H67562An　1986　[E]　　86-45567
ISBN 0-382-09326-7 (lib. bdg.)
ISBN 0-382-09330-5 (pbk.)

**Printed in Spain by Grafos**

**For Oliver**

LET'S READ
TOGETHER

Mary Hoffman

# ANIMAL HIDE AND SEEK

illustrated by Leon Baxter

**Silver Burdett Company**
Morristown, New Jersey

We're off to see the animals!
Our baby hasn't been to the zoo
before, but *we* have.

Mother says we must show Emily
all the animals. I wonder what
she'd like to see first?

"Oh look, there's a zebra!
Look, there, Emily, see that
lovely striped horse?"
"Where?" says Mother. "*I can't see it.*"

"Come and see the giraffe,"
says Jess. "Look, baby,
over there in the trees.
Can you see its long neck?"
"Where?" says Dad. "*I* can't see it."

Next we go where there's lots of water.
"What's in there?" asks Mother.
"Looks like some dirty old logs to me."
I whisper to the baby,
"Can you see the crocodiles?"

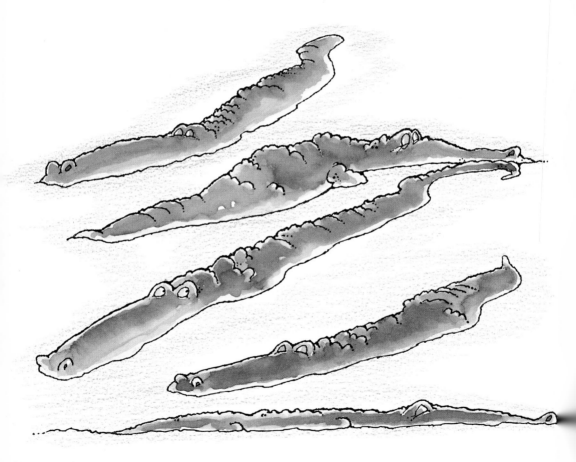

We see some bubbles in a muddy pond.
"Quick, there goes the hippo," says Jess.
But Mother and Dad are too late again.

"Let's go into the reptile house,"
says Dad. "I think I felt some rain."
It's dark inside. Jess and I show Emily
a chameleon on a bright green leaf.

"Hmm," says Dad, "I think this display must be empty. That's a shame!"

Outside the sun is shining brightly again.
We go to see the big cats.
Jess and I show Emily a tiger, a leopard,
and a lion.
Mother and Dad read the signs.

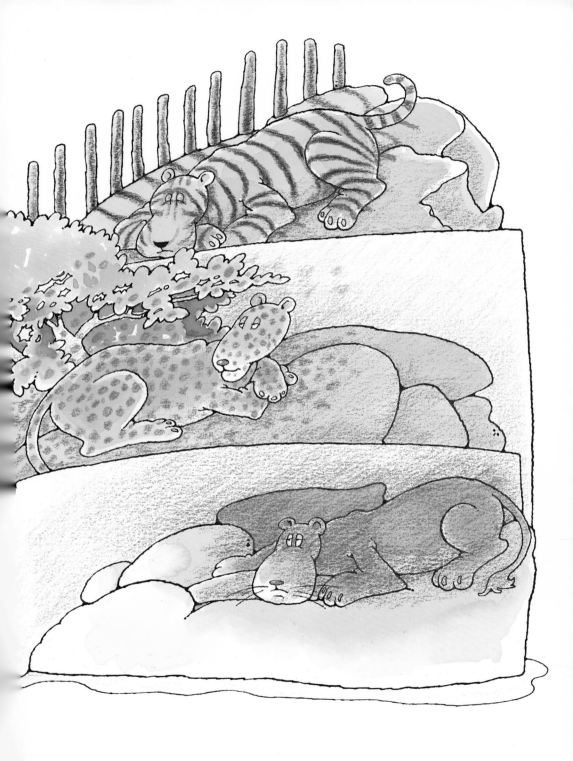

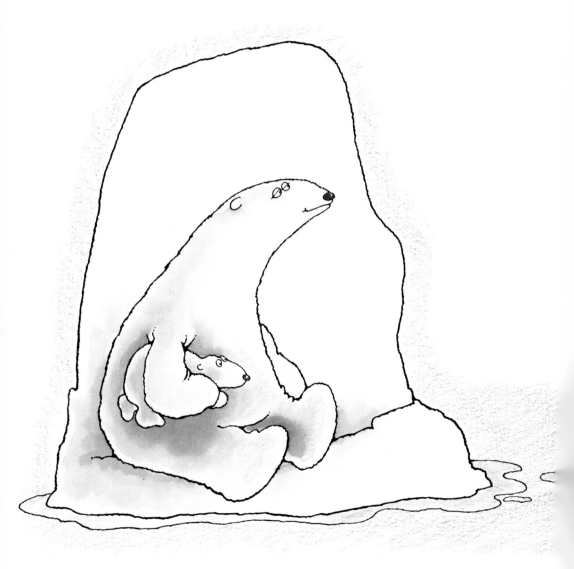

Jess takes us all to see the bears next.
The baby likes the polar bear best.

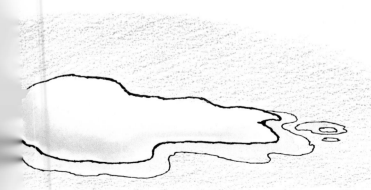

Mother and Dad are getting tired.
"Don't you think we've seen enough
animals for one day?" says Dad.

"But there's another house
we *must* see!" says Jess.

"That's a really pretty sight," says Mother.
"Yes," says Dad. "There's no mistaking a parrot."
So we all saw an animal in the end.